This book belongs to

Designed by Richard Fowler

First published in 1989 by Conran Octopus Limited
37 Shelton Street, London WC2H 9HN

© Conran Octopus Limited

ISBN 1 85029 223 X

Printed in Singapore

Mr Peepers
and the Spotted Wangdoodle

Ruth Thomson

Illustrated by Richard Fowler

Conran Octopus

Mr Peepers, the brave explorer, was reading
his morning newspaper as usual.
"Goodness me!" he exclaimed, when he read in
the competitions page, *Find the Spotted Wangdoodle
and win a big prize*. "That sounds like
a good adventure. But where shall I go?"

He twirled his globe and stuck in a pin.
"The Amazon rainforest," he announced to
Eagle Eye, his dog. "That sounds promising."
He scurried about the house, gathering equipment.
"I hope I haven't forgotten anything," he said.

BIG PRIZE!
Find the
Spotted
Wangdoodle
Competition!

Last known photograph.

Some weeks later, Mr Peepers and Eagle Eye
were paddling down the Amazon river.
"Aha!" he said, glimpsing some strange spots
among the trees. "I wonder if that's the
Spotted Wangdoodle?"

was it?

No, it was
It was Pab
"Excuse m
"have you

The boy smiled and nodded.
Beckoning to Mr Peepers, he leapt up and ran
into the undergrowth.
"What luck," said Mr Peepers, following him.

Mr Peepers stumbled and crawled through the tangled forest. The boy was out of sight. Nearby he could hear a loud rumbling.

e could see something spotted.
Spotted Wangdoodle," he said,

s he right?

No, he **was**
It was **a sle**
"Ssh," **said**
as they **tipt**
and **deeper**

"Now where's he going?" muttered Mr Peepers,
as the boy disappeared up a tree. "Perhaps the
Spotted Wangdoodle lives in the treetops."
He scrambled up as well.

d, looking through his binoculars.

was it?

No, it was **not**.
It was a great **bi**
Mr Peepers **was**
the Spotted **War**

He crawled
was pointing
and ... broke

downwards. Pablo peered through
re he had gone. There was
e could see something spotted.

ted Wangdoodle at last?

No, it wa
It was a b
a flower

Luckily, Mr Peepers had a soft landing,
but he was feeling rather dizzy from his fall.
He saw spots wherever he looked.

When Mr Peepers recovered, he noticed some
rare spotted beetles on a nearby tree trunk.
"I must have a picture of these," he said.

oking at the beetles,
ablo silently pointing at a hole
him. *What* was that inside?

e Spotted Wangdoodle?

Yes, it was!

Mr Peepers did, of course, win the prize.
"How daring you are," said everyone. "How brave!"
"How clever you are," said everyone. "What skill!"
"It was nothing, really," replied Mr Peepers, shyly.
"It was all a big mistake."

Nobody believed him.
But we know the truth, don't we?

PRIZE
GIVING ➤➤